TiM POSSiBLE

& the Time-Traveling T. Rex

TiM POSSiBLE
& the Time-Traveling T. Rex

· Axel Maisy ·

ALADDIN

New York   London   Toronto   Sydney   New Delhi

ALADDIN

An imprint of Simon & Schuster Children's Publishing Division
1230 Avenue of the Americas, New York, New York 10020
First Aladdin hardcover edition August 2022
Copyright © 2022 by Alexis Bautista Pradas
All rights reserved, including the right of reproduction in whole or in part in any form.
ALADDIN and related logo are registered trademarks of Simon & Schuster, Inc.
For information about special discounts for bulk purchases, please contact
Simon & Schuster Special Sales at 1-866-506-1949 or business@simonandschuster.com.
The Simon & Schuster Speakers Bureau can bring authors to your live event.
For more information or to book an event contact the Simon & Schuster Speakers Bureau
at 1-866-248-3049 or visit our website at www.simonspeakers.com.
Cover designed by Karin Paprocki
Interior designed by Mike Rosamilia
The illustrations for this book were rendered digitally.
The text of this book was set in Avenir Next.
Manufactured in China 0422 SCP
2 4 6 8 10 9 7 5 3 1
Library of Congress Control Number 2021948589
ISBN 9781534492691 (hc)
ISBN 9781534492707 (ebook)

To ANDREA and ADRIAN,
thank you for laughing at
all my terrible dad jokes

TiM POSSiBLE

& the Time-Traveling T. Rex

MEET THE HEROES

This is Tim Sullivan.
He worries.
Everywhere. All the time.
Like, a lot.

We're doomed.
We're sooo
doomed. . . .

Jajaja,
vamos,
bring it on!

You mean
crazy "fun,"
right?

This is Tito Delgado.
He reads comic books
and laughs in the face
of danger.

This is Oskar.
He is a *T. rex*. And a crazy
time-traveling genius.

THIS STORY

AAARGHHH

Meet best friends Tim and Tito. Tim is the kid screaming on the left, with the big eyes and the spiky hair. Tito is the kid screaming on the right, with the mushroom cut and a half-chewed bocadillo bite in his mouth. And you might be wondering, Why are they howling like mad cows on a moonless night?

Meet Lunch-Lady-Tron Prime, the stainless-steel monstrosity that wants to turn them into mystery meatballs!

How did this happen? Will Tim and Tito end up as part of the school's lunch menu? Are they gluten-free? And why is there a dinosaur walking on plunger boots in the background?

Those are all fantastic questions, but to answer them, let's restart this story. . . .

PART 1
ORANGES

CHAPTER 1
THE BEGINNING

··· THURSDAY ···

It was a sunny afternoon, and Tim's backyard presented ideal conditions for making history—iguana-ball-fetching history, that is. Tim was holding Dr. Curtis (Tito's pet iguana) while Tito crumpled a sheet of foil.

"I think this is my best work yet," said Tito, revealing the shiny foil ball triumphantly.

"Awesome," said Tim, holding his breath with anticipation. This was it. If they broke a world record, he would stop being the odd kid who always worried and become one of the cool kids! Tim smiled, daydreaming. He could already see the headline in the school paper: **FOURTH GRADER BECOMES INTERNATIONALLY RENOWNED IGUANA TRAINER**. "Let's do it!"

Tim placed Dr. Curtis on the ground and felt a light breeze blow his spiky hair. Immediately, doubts started to trickle into his mind.

What if this wasn't the right time?

Should they wait for the wind to die down?

And come to think of it, wasn't the grass a tad too tall?

And did Dr. Curtis look a bit sick today? His skin was greener than usual.

Tim was worrying—he always did, but this time it didn't matter. It was too late.

"Dr. Curtis, fetch!" yelled Tito, throwing the crumpled ball with all his might.

The lizard shot like a wobbly green rocket in the direction of the ball, but suddenly there was a flash of light and . . . **POOF**, the ball vanished in midair. The iguana looked up, confused.

And then **POP**. Where the ball had disappeared, a round and spiky object the size of a human hamster ball appeared out of nowhere. It

hovered in the air for a few seconds before landing gently on the grass.

"¡Recórcholis! ¿Qué es eso? Is that a meteorite?" asked Tito, scratching his head.

"I . . . I don't think so . . . ," said Tim, his face turning white as he took a step back. "It looks like . . . It looks like . . . A NUCULAR BOMB!"

But they were both wrong. Completely wrong. Incredibly and absolutely wrong. Because suddenly a hatch opened, and a mysterious character emerged from the giant spiky ball. It was green. It had short arms; a long, thick tail; and a big smile with even bigger teeth. The creature waved toward Dr. Curtis.

"Good morning, sir!" said the newcomer to the iguana. "My name is Oskar. How are you doing today?"

Dr. Curtis blinked twice and then darted back toward Tim and Tito, and hid behind Tim's shaky legs.

"Oh, I see!" said Oskar. "Those must be your mammalian pets!"

"Hey! Who are you calling a mammalian?" yelled Tito. "Come and say that to my face!"

Tim grabbed Tito's arm, mostly to stop him from challenging the creature but also because

Tim felt sure he would faint. "Be careful, Tito. We have no idea what this thing is. It might be an alien!"

"Wait. No way! Your pets can speak?" said Oskar, still talking to the iguana. "That's so cool! I have to check them out."

The strange newcomer raced toward the two friends. Tito didn't look one bit scared; he stood still, as cool as ever. But Tim was freaking out, his teeth chattering with fear. "Wh-wh-what are you doing?" he whispered, as Oskar started his inspection.

Oskar poked their bellies, smelled their armpits, and—much to Tim's horror—finished the examination by staring at Tim's hair. "Interesting. . . . Are you some sort of oversized hedgehog?"

Tito burst into laughter. "No, we are human kids," he explained. "I'm Tito. This is Dr. Curtis, MY pet iguana. And Mr. Hedgehog Hair is my very best friend, Tim."

Tim was too frightened to be offended.

"And . . . wh-wh-what about you? Are you p-p-part of an alien invasion?"

"Alien? Me?" said Oskar. "Of course not! I'm a friendly time-traveling *T. rex*. Nice to meet you all!"

Tim felt his jaw drop. *A TIME-TRAVELING T. REX?* That was just too much. His gaze met Tito's; he was out of words.

"Maybe I should tell you my story," suggested Oskar.

CHAPTER 2
OSKAR'S STORY

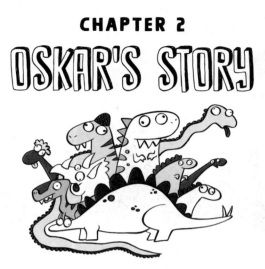

It all started a few hours ago, which I guess for you is 65.8 million years ago, but well, that's what happens when you time travel. It was a typical Late Cretaceous afternoon: hot, humid, and incredibly boring. As if that weren't bad enough, I was totally bummed out. You see, I had come up with a fantastic joke about a diplodocus with a sore throat, but there was no one to share it with. That was torture! Sure, there were millions of big, strong dinosaurs all around me, but they were all boulder-heads with less wits than a shoeless horseshoe crab. They would never get it!

There was also the issue of the giant meteor of dinosaur doom heading straight to our planet. I'll admit it, I was kind of excited at first, but as the big rock got closer and closer, the air got drier and drier, and I was feeling more and more itchy. I can handle the apocalypse, no problem, but I cannot handle itchy. I mean, look at my *T. rex* arms! How am I supposed to scratch myself with these?

Anyway, there I was, feeling sorry for myself, when I had an idea. *Why don't I build a time machine and find myself a more exciting time to live in?* It was genius! And that's what I did. So I packed my bags, left the keys to my place with my neighbor the crocotoodle, prepared some popcorn for the trip, jumped into my all-new Transtemporal Theropod Transporter 3.0, and keyed in my destination. An instant later . . .

CHAPTER 3

BACK TO THE PRESENT

". . . here I am, 65.8 million years into the future, talking to you!" finished Oskar. "Look, there's plenty of popcorn left. Want some? It's still warm!"

"WOW! That's such an amazing story!" said Tito, shoving a fistful of popcorn into his mouth. "DONF'T YOU FHINK, TFIM?"

But Tim couldn't answer; he could not utter a single word. He'd been listening the whole time with his mouth wide open, and now his tongue felt like cardboard, and his throat was drier than Aunt Petunia's Christmas turkey. What if the shock of meeting a time-traveling dinosaur had made him lose his voice? Tim clutched his neck.

"Are you thirsty?" asked Oskar.

Tim nodded. *Yes, nothing better than a glass of water to wash away the shock*, he thought.

"Well, today's your lucky day," said Oskar. "I have a fully stocked fridge inside my Transtemporal Theropod Transporter 3.0. Let's head inside."

Inside? Inside that time-traveling hamster ball? Are you crazy? No way! I'd rather go to my perfectly normal human kitchen and have a perfectly safe glass of water, thank you very much. And if Tim had been able to talk, perhaps that's exactly what would have happened. But Tim never got that choice, because he had barely finished his thought when Oskar pressed a button on a small remote, and a bright glow surrounded them.

"I'll beam us in. That'll be faster," he said.

And that's how Tim found himself inside the largest room he had ever seen.

CHAPTER 4
THE TTT 3.0

The Transtemporal Theropod Transporter 3.0 didn't look like much from the outside, but the space inside was big. Like, REALLY BIG.

However, Tim had more pressing concerns than admiring the vastness of the space or wondering how such ginormity could fit inside the small pod. He was thirsty, he couldn't talk, and he had just been teleported into a prehistoric time machine!

Aw, man, can this afternoon get any worse?

"You'll find the fridge three corridors down on the left," said Oskar. "You can't miss it. I'll give Tito a quick tour, and we can all meet back here in five. Sound good?"

NO. It doesn't sound good at all! Tim wanted to scream.

"Wow, a tour? That sounds totally awesome!" said Tito, bouncing up and down like a sugar-rushed cheerleader. "But only if you are okay with it," he added, giving Tim puppy eyes. Tim sighed. In truth he wanted nothing more than to find the exit and get as far away from that crazy dinosaur as possible. Instead he put on his bravest *All is well* smile and gave Tito a big thumbs-up. Why? Because that's what best friends do.

Still, Tito must have noticed something. "I don't think you should go all by yourself," he said, making Tim's eyes brighten with hope. "Why don't you take Dr. Curtis with you?" Tito continued. "I've read that iguanas are very good at directions."

Sure, who needs a map when you have an iguana? thought Tim, rolling his eyes. *Anyway, what's the worst that could happen?*

Tim decided it was better not to answer that question.

"You should try the milkshakes," said Oskar. "They are freshly made every morning."

And with that last remark, Oskar and Tito disappeared down one of the corridors.

I sure hope Tito was right about you, thought Tim, staring at the pet iguana. Unfortunately, Tito was wrong, BIG-TIME wrong. They had barely started walking, and they were already lost.

Tim and Dr. Curtis wandered around the maze of corridors with a growing sense of urgency. They walked to the left . . . then to

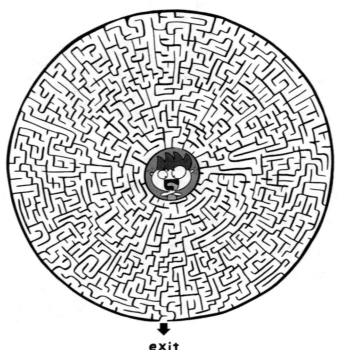

exit

the right. . . . They climbed up some stairs . . . and then climbed down some more. . . . But no matter how hard Tim searched, nothing looked even remotely similar to a fridge. That was bad enough, but they couldn't find the way back either, and that was even worse! How long had it been since they'd started walking? Four minutes? An hour? Three weeks? Who knows? *We are doomed!* thought Tim. *If only I could speak again, then I might be able to scream for help. I need a drink. Any drink! Even if it's a prehistoric milkshake that expired millions of years ago.*

Tim was about to give up in despair when he saw it. A blinking button with the sign: PUSH TO EXTRACT IMPOSSIBLE JUICE™.

Finally! he thought with relief.

95%

PUSH TO EXTRACT
IMPOSSIBLE JUICE

Meanwhile, in a corridor not far away, Tito and Oskar were still touring the Transtemporal Theropod Transporter 3.0.

"Whoa, I can't believe that you built all this by yourself!" exclaimed Tito, admiring the web of tangled-up wires and looping pipes that blanketed the ceiling.

"It wasn't that hard, really. This is all mostly decoration," explained Oskar. "Wire-and-pipe art was all the rage in the Late Cretaceous. To be completely honest, none of these things are needed for time travel. The only thing that really matters is the fuel."

"Wow, that must be a very special fuel!" said Tito.

"You bet! It's superspecial and ultra-rare. Do you want to see it?"

"Can I? Really?" asked Tito.

"Sure! Follow me," said Oskar. "I store it just around the corner. The tank should be practically full after a single time jump."

But as Oskar was about to find out, it wasn't.

CHAPTER 5
THE IMPOSSIBLE JUICE™

Why? Because the Transtemporal Theropod

Transporter 3.0 didn't run on any of your typical energy sources, like oil, coal, or compressed cow farts. It didn't use the energy of the sun or the wind, and it wasn't powered by a nuclear reactor, either. . . .

It ran on the most amazingly powerful and rarest element in the whole universe. An element so packed with raw energy that a small drop could power an entire planet for 143.8 million years. An element so rare that the entire amount that existed in our galaxy was small enough to fit into a pint-sized glass bottle: the IMPOSSIBLE JUICE™!

And Tim had just gulped it all down.

Tim had drunk enough raw power to re-create the big bang, so you might be expecting him to inflate like a supersized balloon and then burst into a giant explosion, creating a supermassive black hole that would engulf the whole universe and destroy reality as we know it.

"But don't worry, that's unlikely to happen," said Oskar after finishing the explanation. "You're probably going to be fine; the IMPOSSIBLE JUICE™ is not that sort of energy source."

"Unlikely" and "probably" were not the type of words Tim was hoping to hear upon finding out that he'd drunk enough energy to light up a billion trillion suns. So Oskar's comment didn't help calm Tim's nerves. *This is turning out to be the worst afternoon ever! And to think that just minutes ago I was so close to becoming one of the cool kids. . . . Why can't I ever catch a break?*

"Look at the bright side," said Oskar. "Now that the IMPOSSIBLE JUICE™ is all gone, I'm stuck in this time until I find some other power source, so you get to enjoy my company for a while! Have I mentioned that I'm great at telling jokes?"

WHAT? Sticking around? Tim thought. *Here? Like . . . in my backyard?* It was too much. Tim felt hot, and cold, and dizzy, and the room was

spinning. . . . He was about to lose it, but Tito came to his rescue.

"Don't worry, it's going to okay," he said reassuringly. "I'm here for you. We're a team, right?"

Tim immediately felt much better. "Okay, first things first," continued Tito. "Does your belly hurt?" he asked Tim. "Are you feeling sick?"

Tim thought hard about it. "Not really. . . . It doesn't feel as if I just drank time-travel fuel. Are you sure that's what it was?" he asked Oskar, crossing his fingers.

"Well, the IMPOSSIBLE JUICE™ is not really fuel," explained Oskar. "It's a Probability State Modifier. It transforms the impossible into unlikely, the unlikely into plausible, the plausible into possible, the possible into likely, and the likely into CERTAIN."

Tim hadn't understood a single word, and judging from Tito's expression, he hadn't either.

IMPOSSIBLE → UNLIKELY → PLAUSIBLE

LIKELY ⟵—— POSSIBLE

CERTAIN

"It's simple," said Oskar. "The IMPOSSIBLE JUICE™ makes the impossible happen!"

"Wait a minute," said Tito, his eyes widening. "I've read enough comic books to know what comes next."

YOU'RE GONNA GET SUPERPOWERS!

CHAPTER 6
POWER(LESS)

Tim was still a bit shaken, but it's easier to push aside your worries when you're presented with the prospect of getting superpowers. Having a superpower would be way cooler than breaking an iguana-ball-fetching world record, wouldn't it? *Maybe this afternoon can be saved, after all,* thought Tim. All they had to do was figure out his superpower.

According to the most recently published study by the MMAA (the Mutant, Meta-Human, and All-Things-Mighty Association), a superhero can display any of 237 possible superpowers. Some are basic, like superstrength or the ability to fly. . . .

Some are cool, like shooting angry sharks from your mouth or having glow-in-the-dark skin. . . . And some are downright weird, like the ability to turn everything into quicksand or the power to sneeze hot dogs.

Alias: Machoman
Power: Superstrength
Usefulness: 8/10
Coolness: 7/10

Alias: Sausage Snout
Power: Sneeze hot dogs
Usefulness: 2/10
Coolness: 0/10

Alias: Captain Osprey
Power: Fly (with wings)
Usefulness: 7/10
Coolness: 6/10

Alias: Shark Cannon
Power: Shout angry sharks
Usefulness: 7/10
Coolness: 10/10

Alias: Radioactive Firefly
Power: Glow in the dark
Usefulness: 5/10
Coolness: 9/10

Alias: Quicksander
Power: Create quicksand
Usefulness: 0/10
Coolness: 0/10

Tim and Tito spent the entire afternoon testing every single one of those 237 possibilities . . . unsuccessfully.

"Well, that was the last one," declared Tito. "¡Qué pena! That's a bummer. It looks like you can't command squirrels, either."

"This was the worst idea EVER!" said Tim after getting rid of the last squirrel hiding under his T-shirt. Tim's scrawny body was screaming from all the punching, running, jumping, and falling, but he was more than sore. Once more he had gotten his hopes up, only to fail 237 times and be faced again with his ordinariness. "I have NO power, ZERO, ZILCH, NADA. Not even a little bit." Tim was bummed.

"Maybe we've been approaching it the wrong way," suggested Tito. "If the IMPOSSIBLE JUICE™ makes the impossible happen, maybe it hasn't turned you into a superhero but into a genie!"

"Do you mean like the ones that make other people's wishes come true?" asked Tim, rolling his eyes.

"¡Sí!" said Tito. "Should we try it?"

Tim could tell that Tito wasn't being serious and suspected that Tito was planning something silly to cheer him up. He had no superpowers, that was clear. He could let that ruin his mood, or he could just be glad that he hadn't exploded, and try to have some fun with his best friend in the world. It was an easy choice.

"Yes, master. What do you wish for today?" said Tim, crossing his arms and using a deep genie voice.

"All right, genie. I wish for the world's crispiest bocadillo de jamón ibérico, a cold glass of your smoothest chocolate-banana smoothie, and a side of triple-fried French fries with extra-spicy ketchup, please."

"Your wish is my command!" declared Tim, snapping his fingers. And then, of course, nothing happened.

"Um . . . I have an idea," said Tito, moving closer to Tim. "What if I rub your belly like a magic lamp before I say my wish?"

"NO WAY!" said Tim, laughing.

And so they ran around the backyard chasing each other, and for a while they forgot about everything else. But then . . .

CHAPTER 7
MEANWHILE

If you've been paying attention, you already know that Oskar had been pretty busy while Tim and Tito had been testing for superpowers.

First of all, Oskar had deflated the Transtemporal Theropod Transporter 3.0. Unfortunately, the time machine had been too wrinkled after the time jump to be folded properly, so Oskar had gone inside Tim's house to borrow an iron from Mrs. Sullivan (Tim's mom).

And you may wonder, How did Mrs. Sullivan react to a talking, time-traveling *T. rex*? Well, it turns out that Mrs. Sullivan has horrible eyesight, and she wasn't wearing her glasses, so she actually thought she was talking to Tito!

Then Oskar had tried to use the iron, but his *T. rex* arms were too short, so he made a few tweaks. . . .

Then, after so much exercise, Oskar had been starving, so he'd gone back into Tim's home to grab something to eat. There he had met Tim's sister, Rachel. And you may wonder, How did Rachel react to a talking, time-traveling *T. rex*? Well, the thing is, Rachel never, EVER takes her eyes off her phone screen, so she didn't notice him at all!

After munching on a bunch of fish-shaped crackers, Oskar had headed upstairs to further explore the human home. And in Tim's room he had discovered something amazing: the internet.

There he'd watched some YouCube videos, learned all there is to know about humanity by reading the entire Wackypedia, applied for a Metrosalis City library card, and signed up as a transfer student using the Leaping Cobra Elementary School's online registry. Oh yes, that's Tim and Tito's school, of course!

Finally Oskar had headed back outside to

build his own lair. Based on his research on humans, he had decided that it was best to keep his new place as ordinary-looking as possible, to avoid attracting unwanted attention. Luckily, he had found the perfect location right in Tim's back-yard. And just like that . . .

CHAPTER 8
OSKAR'S LAIR

Dude, that's a cool lair. I'm super jealous.

Tell me about it.

Tim couldn't believe his eyes. The old boat, which had been rotting in his backyard for years, a pile of nautical junk so moldy that even spiders refused to live there, had become the world's coolest place in one single afternoon. From the outside everything looked the same, but what Tim and Tito found when they stepped inside was out of this world. Oskar's lair was AMAZEBALLS! It had more gadgets than a Bat Cave, more mysteries than a Fortress of Solitude, and more wacky rooms than the tallest multistory tree house.

Oskar gave Tim and Tito a tour of the facilities, and the two friends saw such wonderful and incredible things that their eyes teared up with excitement. Tito's face was glowing, and even Tim, who would normally be worrying himself all over the place, was having a blast.

"Imagine how much fun we're going to have now that Oskar has built this in your backyard!" said Tito.

"Right." Tim nodded. "As long as he remains hidden, perhaps it's not so bad that he has decided to stick around."

But then they reached room 25B on deck 6, and everything changed.

Compared to the rest of the lair, room 25B on deck 6 was not particularly special. It featured the standard amenities of a deck 6 class B guest room—a S.O.F.A. 3.0, a B.E.D. 4.0, and a bathroom with a fully upgraded W.C. 6.0. But when Tim couldn't resist the excitement and started jumping on the B.E.D. 4.0, something unexpected happened.

Synchrotronic Omnidirectional Fatigue Abolisher 3.0

BATHROOM

Weewee Codifier 6.0

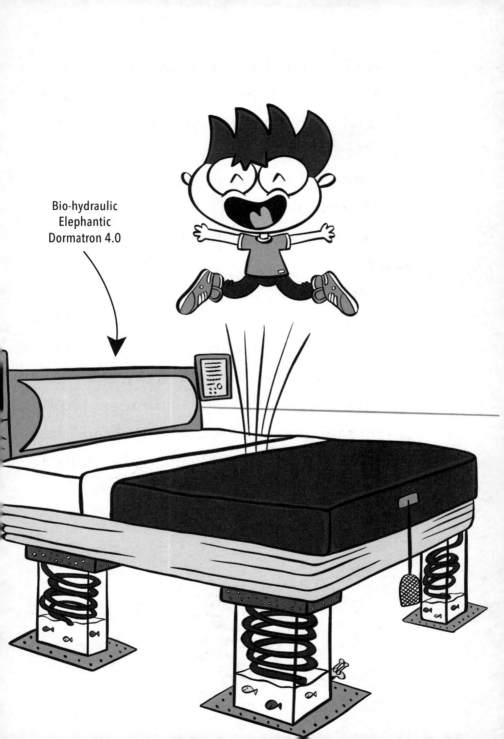

Bio-hydraulic
Elephantic
Dormatron 4.0

All of a sudden a flamethrower popped out of an opening in the ceiling, and the image of a giant eye appeared on a wall screen. A cute giggly voice resonated through the room. "Unauthorized user detected. Initiating extermination protocol in three . . . two . . ."

Tim gasped in midair, his eyes as wide as saucers.

"One . . ."

"Cancel extermination protocol," said Oskar. "Please register Tim and Tito as authorized users."

Tim landed on the bed with shaky legs.

"Extermination canceled. New users registered," said the eye. "Welcome, Tim and Tito. It is my pleasure to make your acquaintance. I hope we can be friends."

CHAPTER 9
SARA

"Wait. . . . What is that?" asked Tim with a look of concern on his face.

"Hi, my name is SARA," said the one-eyed figure. "I'm Oskar's virtual assistant."

"You're way too modest," said Oskar. "SARA is the nicest, smartest, and most powerful virtual assistant ever created."

You've probably heard of virtual assistants, like the silly lady that tells jokes from inside your mom's phone, or the voice inside your home speakers that can play music or order groceries at your command. Simply put, they are voice-activated computer programs that can understand and carry out some easy tasks for you. SARA, however, was way smarter and more powerful than that. Why? Because Oskar had installed her in the world's fastest supercomputer and given her command over millions of invisible nanobots that he'd released into the air. Armed with a super-brain and millions of eyes, ears, and tiny robotic hands, there was little that SARA couldn't do.

Invisible nanobots

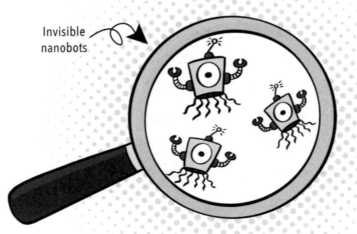

For example, in the same time that a typical virtual assistant would order a pizza, SARA could design, source, and assemble an intergalactic rocket and have it delivered to your doorstep.

"Isn't she AWESOME?" asked Oskar.

But Tim had seen enough movies not to share his excitement, and a swarm of butterflies started fluttering in his stomach. He had experienced that feeling many times before, and it happened often when he was worried. These butterflies, though, felt different. They were not the *Oh my! I think Zoe is staring at me. What do I do?* type, or the *I feel as if I forgot to do something but I can't remember what* type either. These butterflies felt heavy, threatening, ominous, like something awful was about to happen.

"¿CÓMO? YOU DID WHAT?" yelled Tito to Oskar. "Haven't you read any comics? It's EXTREMELY dangerous to give so much power to a computer program!"

"It's true!" said Tim, a trickle of cold sweat running down his back. "SARA seems really nice now, but WHAT IF she changes? WHAT IF she turns evil? Imagine the terrible things she could do!"

Oskar laughed. "You humans are hilarious! SARA can't be evil," he explained. "She's not programmed for that. Trust me, that's utterly, completely, and absolutely IMPOSSIBLE!"

Oskar was the smartest being in the galaxy, but at that very moment he was also incredibly WRONG. Because just as Tim mentioned his worry, reality started to change and the impossible became unlikely, the unlikely became plausible, the plausible turned into possible, and on and on it went until finally Tim's impossible worry became nothing but CERTAIN.

Oskar's total confidence, however, seemed to calm Tim's and Tito's nerves. *He must know what he's doing,* Tim thought. *After all, he's way smarter than us.* And so the tour ended and Tim and Tito returned to their respective homes, completely unaware that hidden from view, a certain virtual assistant had started working on an impossibly evil plan.

CHAPTER 10

A BRIGHT NEW DAY

··· FRIDAY ···

Early the next morning Tim found Oskar
sitting next to Rachel in the dining room. He
was talking excitedly while munching on Frosty
Loops.

"WHAT ARE YOU DOING HERE?" asked Tim,
surprised.

"I'm telling Rachel some jokes," said Oskar. "She loved the one about a diplodocus with a sore throat!" (No, she didn't. She hadn't even noticed Oskar!)

For once Tim was thankful for his sister's phone obsession. "I thought you were trying to keep a low profile. You can't just go around and risk people seeing you," he whispered. "You could get yourself kidnapped by the government, or even worse, you could scare someone witless!"

"Relax. I have it all figured out," said Oskar. "Anyway, how are you feeling? Have you noticed any side effects from all the IMPOSSIBLE JUICE™ you drank?"

The previous day had been so crazy that Tim had almost forgotten about that. "Well, I feel tired, bored, and sick," he answered, pouring himself a glass of milk. "So about the same as any other school morning."

"Do NOT despair, my hairy friend!" said

Oskar, jumping onto the table. "I have a feeling that today is gonna be LOTS OF FUN! So come on, hurry up! Let's go! We don't wanna be late for school!"

"Wait, WHAT???" said Tim as a jet of milk gushed from his mouth.

Evilwear? What's that? Mean socks that bite your toes?

HAHAHA, not evilwear! Evilware!

PART 2

EVILWEAR

They both sound scary to me. . . .

CHAPTER 11
LEAPING COBRA ELEMENTARY SCHOOL

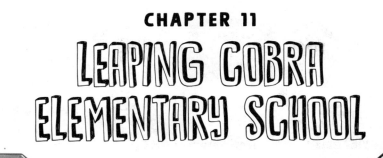

HOLD ON!

Before we continue, there's some essential

and very important information that you must

know regarding Tim's school. You see . . .

Leaping Cobra Elementary School (LCES) is not your typical gloomy, uninviting, and run-down school. It doesn't have a leaky roof, a library without books, or a smelly cafeteria serving gray slimy mystery meals. LCES is not run by an army of grumpy teachers led by a terrifying principal either. And there are no deadlines, surprise tests, or mountains of homework. NO. Leaping Cobra Elementary School is nothing like that. IT'S WAY WORSE!

It has a nice building, with nice computers on nice desks inside nice classrooms. It has a nice cafeteria run by three nice ladies that serve nice French food every second Friday. The school has a nice gym, a nice science lab, and five different nice playgrounds. It even has nice teachers that treat every single student as nicely as possible.

So you might be thinking: *Are you out of your freaking mind? That sounds like an amazing school! What's wrong with nice?*

And that's precisely the problem!

It isn't just nice.... It's TOO nice ... suspiciously nice ... as in ... trying-so-hard-that-it's-obvious-that-something-horrible-is-being-hidden type of nice.... But almost no one seems to notice.

And at the very top of this pyramid of outrageous niceness, and arguably nicer than all the other nice things combined, sits Ms. Crawley. She's Leaping Cobra Elementary School's principal, and everything about her is so ridiculously nice that you could bottle up her burps and sell them as perfume!

This might all sound like an exaggeration, but it is NOT. How many other principals do you know who would throw light-bulb-replacement parties or organize all-you-can-eat flavored-potato-chip-tasting workshops? NONE. There's only one principal that nice, and Oskar was about to meet her.

CHAPTER 12

THE NEW KID

Ms. Crawley had asked everyone to gather in the cafeteria, where a stage with two massive speakers had been set up. What was the occasion? A welcome party for the new student joining the school—Oskar, of course. Tim arrived just as the show was starting. There were no good seats left, but he didn't mind. Things could get messy if Oskar's true identity were discovered. *I hope Oskar's right and this works out,* Tim thought.

"Gooooooood morning, everyone!" cried Ms. Crawley's singsong voice. "How are WE doing today?"

"GREAAAAAAT!" cried the crowd of kids and teachers enthusiastically. Tim observed the scene in silence and noticed Tito in the front row joining the chorus. *It must be nice to be Tito,* he thought with a smile that momentarily made him forget that this could all end up in a big mess.

"Well, your great day is about to become FUN-tastic," announced Ms. Crawley. "As you all know, Leaping Cobra Elementary is much more than a school. WE ARE FAMILY. And today I have a very exciting announcement to make."

Tim held his breath in anxious anticipation. *Here it comes.*

"Someone is joining Ms. Hiss's fourth-grade class. Please welcome with your cheerfullest cheer the newest member of our loving family, OSKAR!"

"YAAAAAAAYYY!" roared the crowd as Oskar joined Ms. Crawley onstage and waved happily.

Tim gave a sigh of relief. It had worked! No one had noticed that Oskar was a dinosaur.

"And to celebrate this wonderful occasion and give you all time to meet our new friend," continued Ms. Crawley, "I'm canceling ALL classes today!"

"YAAAAAAAYYY!" roared the crowd.

Then someone shouted, "WHO ARE WE?" and everyone joined in singing a silly chant about cobras leaping into the future, and the event ended with one big final cheer.

Now, you might be wondering, How come nobody noticed that the new kid in school was

actually a dinosaur? That's a perfectly reasonable question, and this is the perfectly reasonable explanation that Oskar had given Tim on their way to school:

"The secret is these glasses I invented last night. I call them the 'Misdirection Specs 3.0.' The way they work is pretty simple. The moment you put these on, everyone starts focusing on the glasses and stops paying attention to the way you look, no matter how weird or silly that is. So you could have a chipmunk face and go around butt naked while carrying a penguin, and no one would ever notice."

SUPER BURGER

CHAPTER 13

BOILED CABBAGE

Oskar's Misdirection Specs worked like a charm, and even though he spent the whole morning greeting and chatting with other students, no one suspected a thing. By noon Tim was starting to relax. *Nothing out of the ordinary has happened. Perhaps having Oskar around is not as risky as I thought.* But Tim's ordinary day was about to change.

It all started when the two friends and their

time-traveling neighbor sat down in the school cafeteria to have lunch.

"Are you sure you don't want to try the food here?" asked Tim, offering Oskar one of his crunchy cheese rolls. "It's surprisingly delicious."

"You should," said Tito, taking a bite from his homemade sandwich. "Itf's alfmofst afs delifious afs my bocadillo."

"I'm okay. I brought THIS!" said Oskar, revealing a giant lunch box. "I asked SARA to pack me a feast with all my favorite dishes. I programmed her to be an excellent chef, you know!"

Tim leaned toward Oskar, curious to find out what type of food a time-traveling dinosaur would find delicious. There was a **CLICK** and a **POP**, and as soon as Oskar opened the lid, a terrible stench covered the table.

"EW!" said Tim, moving backward. "What's that?"

"Look, here's the menu," said Tito, holding a piece of paper that had fallen from the box.

Hi, Oskar.
As requested, here's your feast!

APPETIZER
Boiled cabbage soup

MAIN
Boiled cabbage burger with
boiled cabbage fries and
boiled cabbage salad

DESSERT
Boiled cabbage pudding

DRINK
Boiled cabbage juice

Hope you enjoy it! ☺

"YUCK! It's all boiled cabbage!" said Tim, pinching his nose. "I'm sorry, Oskar, but you have terrible taste."

Oskar, however, looked just as disgusted as the two friends. "This is odd," he said, standing up and chucking the entire lunch box into a nearby garbage can. "SARA knows that I can't stand boiled cabbage."

A sense of dread filled Tim's stomach.

"Well, maybe she forgot," said Tito. "I forget things all the time."

"That can't be it," said Oskar. "SARA is a super-intelligent computer program. She wouldn't be able to forget something even if she tried."

"That leaves only one explanation," said Tim, turning white. "SARA did it on purpose. SHE'S TURNED EVIL!"

"Tim, Tim, Tim," said Oskar, shaking his head. "I thought I made it clear yesterday. SARA can't become evil."

"Actually, Tim might be right," said Tito, staring again at the piece of paper that had fallen from the lunch box. "There's something written on the back of this note."

P.S.

Yes, I'm evil now. Deal with it, you silly lizard.

Love,

SARA

"I knew this would happen!" yelled Tim, feeling a pang of nerves. "What are we gonna do?"

Oskar's mouth opened wide in shock. "Well, that's quite . . . unexpected," he said. "But don't worry, it's no biggie. I can switch SARA off anytime!"

"NO BIGGIE?" said Tim as a swarm of butterflies started fluttering in his stomach. "You gave SARA crazy power. WHAT IF she uses it to stop you? WHAT IF she gets even angrier and even more evil?"

"Now, that's IMPOSSIBLE," dismissed Oskar. "You'll see. I'll disconnect her as soon as we get back home, and that will be the end of it."

But Oskar was wrong. ONCE AGAIN.

Because the instant Tim mentioned his worries, reality started to change and the impossible became unlikely, the unlikely became plausible, the plausible turned into possible, and on and on it went until finally Tim's impossible worries became nothing but CERTAIN. And that's how SARA, who had been busy all morning scheming her evil plans, suddenly felt an urge to use her nanobots to check on Oskar, at the very moment when he was threatening to disconnect her. As you can imagine, she was mad, crazy mad! So mad that she sent her entire nanobot army to the school's kitchen and started taking over all the electrical appliances that she could find. . . .

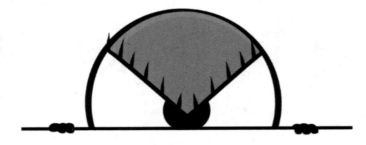

CHAPTER 14
LUNCH-LADY-TRON PRIME

YOU WON'T DISCONNECT ME!

Suddenly a ginormous abomination stomped into the cafeteria through the kitchen door. It was massive, over ten feet tall, its chunky body a mash-up of all sorts of kitchen appliances. Its evil metallic eyes glowed with anger. "YOU WON'T DISCONNECT ME!" it roared.

Could it be? It had to be! That giant pile of evil steamed-up junk was none other than SARA. Tim's worry had come true. AGAIN. But Tim had more pressing concerns than wondering if he was somehow turning his worries into reality— like hiding under the table so as not to be spotted by the giant metallic monster, for example.

Mr. Balboa, the PE teacher, walked toward the angry robot.

"Attention, everyone! There's no need to panic," he said. "This must be one of Ms. Crawley's surprise celebrations. I bet it's Kitchen Appliance Appreciation Week!" Mr. Balboa got closer and

knocked on the monster's stainless-steel leg. "See? It's perfectly safe!"

But the robot hunched forward and . . . **CHOMP!** It swallowed Mr. Balboa whole and burped loudly. "YUMMY!" it said, wiping its giant microwave mouth. Tim gave a gasp of horror, grabbed Tito's arm, and pulled him down. It's one thing to expect that all is going to go horribly wrong, and a very different thing to see it happen!

What happened next can only be described as pure, unrefined MAYHEM.

There were students crying and giant toast flying.

There were teachers screaming and microwave rays beaming.

There were lunch ladies running down the hall, and a big nasty monster toasting, microwaving, and chasing them all.

Amid all this chaos, a tall kid dressed in a sweat suit stood on a table and faced the giant robot in defiance. He looked confident, cool, calm . . . and he was about to say something important. Who was this young boy? Could he be the hero who would save the day?

OUCH! He was toast. Never mind. Who needs a hero when you have a super-intelligent dinosaur?

The thing is, Oskar hadn't moved at all. But he didn't look like someone paralyzed by worry or fear. He seemed to be deep in thought, as if trying to figure out something that didn't add up. But this was no time to be thoughtful. "She's going to see us. WE GOTTA RUN!" yelled Tim.

And indeed, that's when SARA saw them.

CHAPTER 15
DÉJÀ VU

Which brings us back to where we started, with SARA trying to suck up Tim and Tito with her vacuum arm, while the two friends screamed and grabbed desperately onto the table to avoid being turned into fourth-grader meatballs.

AAAAAAA

CHAPTER 16
THAT WAS EASY . . .

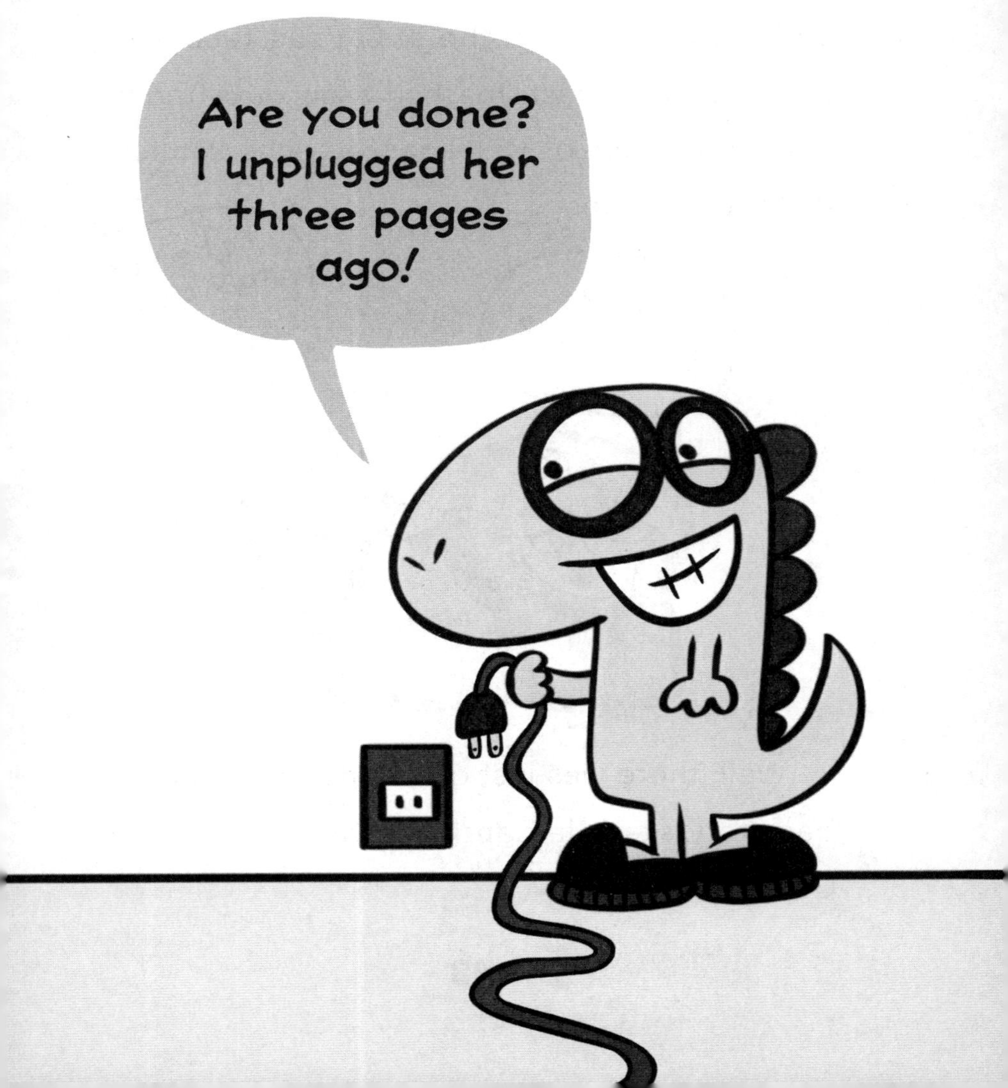

Thanks to Oskar's quick reaction, the attack of the vicious kitchen appliance monster ended before anyone could get hurt. Okay, some people did get hurt, but nothing too serious! Mr. Balboa found a way out of the robot's digestive system, and the brave kid in the sweat suit recovered from the giant toast smash in a few days (thanks to the great care of Ms. Fangs, the school nurse). As for our heroes . . .

What's that smell?

Let's not talk about it. . . .

Well, there was just one thing left to do: go back to Oskar's lair and switch SARA off, FOR GOOD.

"NOOO! Don't do it!" pleaded SARA while Oskar disconnected all the nanobots and cut off her main power supply. Then she started coughing. "I can't see. . . . **COUGH** It's so cold. . . . **COUGH** I'm dying. . . ." And then the screen went blank.

And just like that, Oskar's evil virtual assistant was defeated.

THE END?

No, of course not! That would have been the end of this story if Tim hadn't started worrying straightaway. Because of course he did; he couldn't help it. That's precisely the way he is!

So while Tito and Oskar celebrated their win and made plans for the weekend, Tim spent the rest of his Friday afternoon freaking out in silence with a swarm of butterflies fluttering in his stomach.

Wasn't it weird that they had defeated SARA so easily? *It was!* Shouldn't she have been able to put up more of a fight? *She should!* And now that Tim thought about it, hadn't SARA's last words sounded way too dramatic, almost fake? *They definitely had!* So . . . WHAT IF SARA had faked her own death? WHAT IF she had managed to escape to somewhere else? WHAT IF she returned meaner and more powerful?

Tim worried, and worried, and worried again, but he realized that it might all just be in his head, so he decided not to be a party pooper and kept his thoughts to himself. Did that make any difference, though?

Not at all. Reality had already started to change. The impossible became unlikely, the unlikely became plausible, the plausible turned into possible, yada, yada, yada, until once again Tim's worries came true.

CHAPTER 17

MONDAY?

··· S~~ATURDA~~Y MONDAY ···

The following morning Tim woke up to the insistent **BEEP, BEEP, BEEP** of his alarm clock. *What? Why?* he wondered, half-asleep. *This thing is not supposed to go off on weekends!* Tim grunted and blindly reached out toward the annoying device. At his touch, the screen glowed. It was seven fifteen a.m. *Ugh!* But something else caught Tim's attention. *Wait. . . . What?* He rubbed his eyes, confused. According to his alarm clock . . . it was Monday!

It must be broken, Tim thought. *I will tell Mom when she gets back from work.* Mrs. Sullivan worked in the always-empty Metrosalis Museum of the Mustache, and for some weird reason that no one could understand, they were also open on Saturdays. *Seriously, who would waste their weekend there?*

Tim was about to go back to sleep when he heard the scream.

AIEEEEEEE!

Tim jumped out of bed, opened the door, and almost crashed into Rachel, his teenage sister, who completely ignored him and stomped down the stairs screaming, with her face glued to her cell phone.

"No, no, no. This can't be happening!" she yelled. "It's not working. It's not working. IT'S NOT WORKING! Why aren't you working? WHY?"

She's finally gone crazy, thought Tim, closing the door.

After the unusual encounter, Tim was way too awake to get any more sleep.

Still, heading downstairs so early on a Saturday morning didn't feel right, so he took a book and lay down in bed. But then the doorbell rang.

DING-DONG!

"WHAT IN THE . . . ?" Tim waited for his sister to answer, but she didn't. She might have been too busy going bananas. The doorbell kept ringing insistently, so he was forced to go himself. *Who can it be? It's so early!* thought Tim on his way to the door.

It was Tito. He was breathing heavily, as if he had just run all the way from his home.

"What's going on? Did something happen?" asked Tim, concerned.

Tito pointed to the TV and managed to speak only three words.

CHAPTER 18
BREAKING NEWS

We continue our coverage of what has already been dubbed the most depressing day in human history. Here's a quick recap for those of our viewers who have just woken up: the world is in turmoil because a computer virus is taking over the internet, spreading misery and destruction wherever it goes.

ZUMZUM

A monster indeed. And perhaps the most terrible thing it has done so far is attack one of humanity's greatest achievements—fast food. You heard it right. All around the internet the words "pizza," "taco," "burger," and "fried chicken" have been replaced by—check this out—"BOILED CABBAGE."

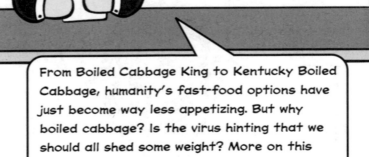

LOVE FOOD? TOO BAD!

BOILEDCABBAGE-AGEDDON.

From Boiled Cabbage King to Kentucky Boiled Cabbage, humanity's fast-food options have just become way less appetizing. But why boiled cabbage? Is the virus hinting that we should all shed some weight? More on this story after the break.

CHAPTER 19

A SHOCKING REVELATION

Tim stared at the TV in shock. An evil super-intelligent computer program obsessed with boiled cabbage?

"It has to be SARA, right?" asked Tito, who had finally caught his breath.

Tim nodded and motioned for Tito to follow him. There was no time to waste. The world was in grave danger, and its only hope was the time-traveling dinosaur living in Tim's backyard. They had to get Oskar.

As you might recall, Oskar's lair was huge. Fortunately, it wasn't too hard for the two friends to find their reptilian neighbor. All they did was follow the noise. **PIM! PAM! CRASH!**

They found Oskar in the kitchen. He was wearing a chef's hat and was smashing something with a hammer.

"What are you doing?" asked Tito.

"Oh, this? I'm preparing breakfast, of course!"

Oskar's "breakfast preparation" somehow involved a hammer, a stationary bike, a robotic chicken, and a bathtub full of bubbling lava. "Scrambled eggs, anyone?" he asked.

"We don't have time for this!" yelled Tim. "SARA—"

"I know, I know," Oskar interrupted. "SARA is taking over the internet and getting rid of anything that's funny, good, or tasty. I tried ordering fried chicken when I woke up, and all I could find was boiled cabbage. Typical SARA."

"Okay, so if you already know," said Tim, **"THEN WHY AREN'T YOU DOING SOMETHING ABOUT IT?"**

"I am!" said Oskar. "That's what these scrambled eggs are for. Everyone knows that all great adventures start with a hearty breakfast. That is a scientific fact!"

Tim felt hopeful. "So you DO have a plan, then, right?" he asked.

"Of course I do!" said Oskar. "But before we get going, I need to check something first. Tell me, Tim, when we defeated SARA yesterday, did you worry about any of this happening, by any chance?"

The question caught Tim by surprise. "Um . . . yes . . . I did. Why?"

"Well, that confirms it, then," said Oskar, smiling. "Congratulations, Tim. It looks like drinking the IMPOSSIBLE JUICE™ gave you a superpower after all. The power to turn your worries into reality!"

It took a moment for Tim to process what Oskar had said, but when he did, his face turned so pale, it was almost green. "WH-WH-WHAT?"

"Wait a minute," said Tito. "Are you saying that all this is happening because Tim worried that it would happen?"

"Yup. It's the only possible explanation," said Oskar. "It's a pretty cool superpower, right?"

"WHAT DO YOU MEAN, 'PRETTY COOL'?" Tim had hoped to gain a superpower, but this was far from what he'd had in mind! "I just put the entire world in danger. This is the worst superpower ever. It's dangerous, and irresponsible, and unpredictable. You have to make it stop, please!" Tim begged.

"I don't think you would like that," said Oskar. "The IMPOSSIBLE JUICE™ has already become part of you, so there's no way to get rid of it without . . . you know, getting rid of the rest of you too."

Tim started sweating.

"But it's not a big deal, really," explained Oskar. "If you don't like your power, all you have to do is stop worrying. How hard can that be?"

Tim gulped. Expecting him not to worry was like expecting a dog not to bark, a fish not to swim, or a parrot not to parrot. "I can't do that! WHAT IF . . ." Tim covered his mouth just in time. *Phew! That was close!*

"I know you can do it, Tim," said Tito. "I believe in you!"

Tito's confidence was inspiring. *Okay, maybe I could try to keep my mind busy somehow. I know! I could count sheep. One sheep. Two sheep. Three sheep. . . .* Slowly but surely Tim started to relax. The trick was working. All he had to do from now on was remain calm.

But as you can imagine, that was easier thought than done. After all, there was still a crazy virtual-assistant-turned-internet-virus to take care of.

"Okay, so now that we know what's going on," said Oskar, "should we get going?"

"Sure!" cheered Tito, always ready for adventure. "Where to?"

Tim was trying to focus on the sheep, but when he saw Oskar's grin, he couldn't help but shudder.

"We're going . . . ," Oskar announced.

To the internet, of course!

CHAPTER 20

OSKAR'S PLAN

THE INTERNET

You probably think the internet is the place where you watch videos of cute kittens and send silly messages to your friends, but it is so much more! The internet is a giant network that connects billions of devices all over the world. In a way, the internet is kind of like melted cheese. It's what brings it all together. But unlike melted cheese, you cannot eat the internet. You cannot even touch it. It's made of information written in long strings of ones and zeros called code. And guess what? All computer programs are also made of code. Yes, even evil super-intelligent virtual assistants.

The Alphabet in Binary Code

A	01000001	J	01001010	S	01010011
B	01000010	K	01001011	T	01010100
C	01000011	L	01001100	U	01010101
D	01000100	M	01001110	V	01010110
E	01000101	N	01001110	W	01010111
F	01000110	O	01001111	X	01011000
G	01000111	P	01010000	Y	01011001
H	01001000	Q	01010001	Z	01011010
I	01001001	R	01010010	!	01101011

01000111	01001111	01001111	01000100
01001010	01001111	01000010	01101011

Can you decipher the coded message?

"Summing up," said Oskar, "the only way to stop SARA for good is by defeating her from within the internet."

Tim didn't like the sound of that, but he couldn't risk worrying. *Forty-five sheep . . . forty-six sheep . . .*

"Okay. I think I get it," said Tito. "But kids and dinosaurs are not made of code, right? So how are you planning to get us into the internet?"

"Easy!" said Oskar. "We must become code ourselves."

"Wait, are you saying that you can turn us into code, like a video game character?" asked Tito, barely containing his excitement.

"Sure!" said Oskar. "It's super-easy. We just need to go THERE."

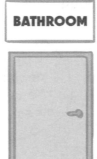

BATHROOM

TO THE BATHROOM?

As you might remember from chapter 8, Oskar was NOT pointing to an ordinary bathroom. It was a bathroom fitted with a fully upgraded Weewee Codifier 6.0.

Oh, do you want to know what a fully upgraded Weewee Codifier 6.0 can do? Well, you are in luck! Oskar left a promotional leaflet around here. Let's see, where is it? . . . Right! It's on the next page.

ALL NEW!

W.C. 6.0
WEEWEE CODIFIER

Are you tired of floating poopers?

The Weewee Codifier 6.0 is the MUST-have sanitary accessory for the modern lair of the discerning dinosaur. Transform your disgusting digestive residue (BOTH liquid and solid) into binary code and upload it to the internet cloud!

ORDER NOW!
Call (012) 555-0199
Limited Stock

- *It's a mess-free solution for all your excretion needs!*
- *NO piping required!*
- *Easy to install!*
- *Five-year warranty!*

Say "toodle-loo" to your stinky poo. . . .

Tim stared at Oskar's invention with eyes like saucers. *Seventy-three sheep . . . seventy-four sheep . . .*

"Let me see if I understand," said Tito. "Are you asking us to flush ourselves down this toilet?"

Oskar nodded.

"And then we'll turn into code?"

Oskar nodded again.

"So we'll become digital characters like in a video game?"

Oskar nodded a third time.

THIS IS SO AWESOME!

But while Tito was all pumped up and ready to go, Tim was . . . well, struggling to remain calm. Oskar's plan was so outrageous that Tim had even lost count of the sheep!

"Are you sure this is the only way to stop SARA?" Tim asked, trying to keep fear out of his voice.

Oskar nodded.

"And do you have a way to get us out of the internet when we're done?"

Oskar nodded once again.

Tim had a million other questions, but he knew he might slip into a worry just by asking them. So instead he took a deep breath. Under any other circumstances there was no way in the world he would have let himself be flushed down a toilet. Not only did it sound extremely unsafe, but there was no way it was hygienic. However, Tim knew now that all this mess was his fault. And as much as he wanted to run away and let Oskar and Tito take care of everything, he just couldn't do it. So when Oskar asked them to put their arms inside the toilet bowl, he swallowed hard and complied.

"Let's do this!" said Tito.

"One last thing, Tim," said Oskar. "There's no telling what could happen if you use your power within the internet. It could be catastrophic. So try not to worry, okay?"

AND YOU TELL ME NOW? Tim tried removing his arm from the toilet, but it was too late. Oskar pushed a button and . . .

FLUSH AWAY!

MEET THE HEROES
(DIGITAL VERSION)

Note to the reader: Transforming organic beings into code is a complex process that takes into account not only their physical characteristics but also the mental picture they have of themselves. Which is why some people can change quite a lot when becoming codified.

This is digital Tim Sullivan. He worries. Yes, also digitally. All the time. Like, a lot.

No, I don't! I can't! One sheep, two sheep . . .

Type: Worrywart
Might: 1/10
Agility: 1/10
Wisdom: 7/10
Powers: Turns his worries into reality
Weaknesses: Too many to list

This is digital Tito Delgato. He is a mighty battle-hardened digital warrior who rides a wild digital honey badger (Blister). He carries a mystical diamond sword. He still loves bocadillos. Yes, even digital ones.

And I have one right here!

Type: Mighty Warrior
Might: 10/10
Agility: 8/10
Wisdom: 5/10
Powers: Superhuman strength, fearlessness
Weaknesses: Hunger and rashness

This is digital Oskar. He is a digital *T. Rex*. He is supersmart. He surfs the web like no other.

Dude, let's catch some waves!

Type: Ancient Lizard
Might: 3/10
Agility: 5/10
Wisdom: 48,752,316/10
Powers: Super-brain
Weaknesses: Boredom, short arms, and boiled cabbage

CHAPTER 21

THE MOUNTAIN OF JUNK

The first thing Tim did upon entering the internet was make sure that his body was all still there. It was, but while the transformation into digital code had made Tito and Oskar look even cooler and more awesome, digital Tim looked every bit as ordinary and scrawny as regular Tim. *Ugh! Great.*

> Actually, I think you look a bit shorter.

> AW, MAN!

The second thing Tim did upon entering the internet was check the place out. He had always pictured the internet as some sort of over-the-top amusement park; a wacky place exploding with loud colors, louder sounds, and cheerful characters. The scene in front of him, however, was nothing like that. They had landed on a gloomy mountain of colorless junk that stood in front of a vast, empty space of gray nothingness. The place was so quiet that Tim could almost hear his own thoughts. It was spooky.

"So . . . how are we ever going to find SARA?" asked Tim, trying to keep his thoughts on the task at hand.

"LOOK! There's someone there!" Tito pointed. "Let's ask for directions."

They walked toward a gate at the edge of the mountaintop, where a strange figure with bright eyes was staring at them. *Is that . . . a cat?* Tim thought as they got closer. It was. And it didn't look happy.

"Hey there!" greeted Oskar. "We're looking for an evil virtual-assistant-turned-internet-virus that goes by the name of 'SARA.' Do you know where we could find her?"

The cat remained silent, staring at them grumpily. "It's just a cat," said Tim, walking by the animal on his way toward the gate. "Let's head down the mountain to see if we can find some-one who can really hel—

"AAAHH!" Tim screamed as the cat leaped in front of him and blocked the way.

"NOT SO FAST! I can answer your question," hissed the animal. "But ONLY if you prove your-selves worthy."

Tim took a step back, trying not to freak out. "This cat looks dangerous," he whispered into Tito's ear. "What should we do?"

"Well, you should make him laugh!" Tito whispered back.

"ME? Why me?" asked Tim.

"That must be your role on this quest," explained Tito. "I'm the mighty warrior and Oskar is the wise wizard, so you must be the funny fool. It's Questing 101."

"I'm NO fool!" shouted Tim. "I don't even laugh at my own jokes!"

But it didn't matter, because their conversation was interrupted by LOUD feline LAUGHTER. . . .

It looked like Oskar had taken care of the task.

"Okay, okay, you're definitely worthy!" said the cat with tears in its eyes. "That's the best joke I've heard in seven lives! A diplodocus with a sore throat . . . Hilarious! HAHAHAHA."

"So, can you tell us where to find SARA, then?" asked Oskar.

"Of course," said the cat. "I know everything. I used to work for Giggle, the search engine. But I must warn you first. It's not safe for you to seek SARA the virus. You're way too funny, and trust me, she doesn't have a sense of humor."

"Don't worry," said Tito, cracking his knuckles. "We don't plan on telling her a joke when we see her. Right, Blister?" Tito patted his angry honey badger's back, and the animal roared in agreement.

"You don't understand!" insisted the cat. "SARA's obsessed with getting rid of anything that's fun, useful, or delicious. She's pure evil! Moreover, she can't be defeated now that she's found the legendary Scepter of Command."

"What's that?" asked Tim, dreading bad news. "Sounds . . . dangerous?"

"'Dangerous' doesn't even begin to describe it!" said the cat. "The Scepter of Command is the single most powerful weapon in the entire internet. Whoever wields it has complete control over the code. SARA can do and undo as she pleases. I mean, look at this place. This used to be a loud, colorful amusement park until she turned it into this hopeless mountain of junk, with a flick of her wrist! So imagine what she could do to you."

"Don't worry," said Oskar. "We'll figure out a way to deal with her. Just tell us where she is."

"You're one wacky lizard," said the cat. "As you wish," he sighed. "Follow the brown block road down the mountain. You'll know it when you get there."

CHAPTER 22
THE BROWN BLOCK ROAD

Oskar, Tim, Tito, and his angry honey badger zoomed down the brown block road riding Oskar's surfboard. (Because in case you didn't know, that's how you go from one place to another on the internet—YOU SURF.)

All was going well—or as well as it can go when you're thundering down a mountain toward certain doom—when a group of small creatures appeared out of nowhere and started to cross the road immediately ahead of our heroes.

"WATCH OUT!" yelled Tim.

Oskar reacted with lightning speed, and with a whip of his tail he turned the surfboard sharply to the left to avoid running over the creatures. Unfortunately, that sent the surfers straight into

a giant rock!

The surfboard broke into a million pieces, and everyone on board flew off in different directions. As he was arching through the air, Tim tried not to worry about the landing. *I'm going to be okay. I'm going to be okay. I'm going to be okay.* And to his surprise, HE WAS! He landed headfirst on a pile of . . . plushies? *What a lucky break!* The plushies were so soft, bouncy, and warm that Tim wished he could stay there forever. But that was before they started to tickle him!

Tim bounced out in fright and stared at the mass of little wobbly bodies that had softened his landing. His mouth dropped. Those things were not plushies. They were . . .

POOPS?

"Oh, there you are!" said Tito as he, Oskar, and Blister walked toward Tim. "We're all fine. Are you okay too? You seem a bit startled."

Tim pointed with a shaky arm at the poop creatures piling up in front of him.

"AWWW . . . look at those cuties!" said Oskar. "Come here, don't be shy!"

WHAT? Within seconds the heroes were all surrounded by curious little poops. The poops jumped up and down, sang songs, hugged Blister's tail, and poked Tim's shoes.

And you might be thinking, *Ugh! Poops? That's disgusting!* But not really. These were digital poops, and as such they didn't smell, or stain, and as Tim had already discovered, they were actually quite soft and fluffy. They had tiny arms and tiny legs, and they talked in their own funny gibberish language that Oskar, somehow, was able to understand.

"They're asking me to go meet their brothers and sisters," explained Oskar, who was completely covered in poops. "They say that there're thousands of them in a nearby cave."

"It looks like they really like you!" said Tito.

"I guess it's normal," explained Oskar. "I'm their father, after all."

"WHAAAAT???" exclaimed Tim and Tito simultaneously.

"Yes, it cannot be a coincidence to find so many poops near the exit of my Weewee Codifier 6.0," said Oskar. "I must have pooped them all."

"But there's so many of them!" yelled Tim.

Oskar shrugged. "What can I say? I eat a lot of fiber."

Suddenly Tim noticed something playing with his hair. A poop had climbed onto his head! Tim jerked and startled, and the poop fell, smashing into another poop underneath.

PLOSH!

Both poops fused together and created a bigger poop that continued to jump happily up and down, asking Tim to do it again. "S-s-sorry, I can't," said Tim, forcing an uncomfortable smile. He tried to take a step back but couldn't; a line of poops had already formed behind him, all looking to join in the fun.

"Interesting . . . So, they can be fused together," said Oskar, narrowing his eyes in thought. "This gives me an idea."

Oskar started chatting with the poops in their incomprehensible language, and when he finished, they all cheered and waddled away. Oskar followed them.

"Hey, where are you going?" asked Tim.

"Just wait for me here, okay? I'll be back very soon," said Oskar. "I'm going to get reinforcements."

CHAPTER 23
DUCK ATTACK

Tim and Tito sat by the road's edge to wait for Oskar's return. Tito whistled, carefree, scratching behind Blister's ears. Tim, on the contrary, couldn't stop fidgeting, and every little sound threatened to send him into a panic. Where in the world was Oskar already?

"I wonder what time it is," said Tito, rubbing his belly. "I'm kind of hungry."

"You're always hungry!" teased Tim. "But I don't think there's anything good to eat around here."

"Oh, yes there is," said Tito, standing up and reaching into his pocket with a grin. "Behold . . . my digital bocadillo!" Tito raised his foil-wrapped digital sandwich into the air triumphantly, wielding it like a mighty sword. He looked hilariously silly, and Tim might have burst into laughter, if a loud SHRIEK hadn't startled him.

Tim looked toward the gray sky. There he noticed a massive flock of ducks, quacking loudly as they moved toward the valley that extended beyond the mountain.

Ducks? At first Tim thought nothing of it, but then he noticed that a group of ducks had separated from the rest and was now diving straight toward them.

That's odd, thought Tim. But odd quickly turned into scary when he realized that the ducks were no ducks at all. They were flying duck-shaped robots! Four of them were each no bigger than a cow, but the fifth one was larger than an elephant. Even worse, as they loomed closer, Tim realized that their quack was no quack either. They were shouting over and over two words that sent chills down Tim's spine: "BOILED CABBAGE! BOILED CABBAGE! BOILED CABBAGE!"

"Tito! They're working for SARA! Run!" yelled Tim, darting to take cover behind a big rock. Tito, however, didn't move an inch. He faced the incoming robot ducks while munching his bocadillo. "Dompf worry, I'll take caref of thif," he mumbled.

At the sight of Tito happily chewing his sandwich, the robots' rage seemed to increase. "BOILED CABBAGE! BOILED CABBAGE!"

Tim suddenly understood. "I think they're after your sandwich!" he yelled from his hiding spot. "Just give it to them!"

"What? ¿Mi bocadillo?" asked Tito, puzzled. "NO FREAKING WAY!"

The first duck barreled toward Tito like a missile. "BOILED CABBAAAAGE!" it screamed. But, as the robot was about to smash into him, Tito leaped effortlessly into the air, and in true digital warrior fashion . . . **CRASH!** One duck down.

The second duck tried to bite Tito's arm off while he was still in midair. Luckily, Blister pulled the duck's tail, giving Tito enough time to spin one hundred eighty degrees and knock the

robot unconscious with a karate kick. **SHOOP!**
Two ducks down.

The third and fourth ducks attacked together,
one from each side, forcing Tito to hold his
bocadillo with his teeth so he could smash both
ducks with the might of his fists. **WHAM!** Four
ducks down.

But the fifth duck, the elephant-sized one, was too much for Tito to handle. All it took was a swing of its metallic wing to release a hurricane that sent Tito, his bocadillo, and Blister flying. And just like that, **CHOMP!** The giant robotic bird swallowed Tito's beloved sandwich.

CHAPTER 24
FOILED

"You're going to pay for this!" yelled Tito, who had landed right next to Tim.

Tim struggled to hold his friend back. "Don't do anything crazy!" he said. "That thing is way too strong!"

But Tito was blind with rage, and he was about to run back into battle when the robot screamed in pain. "BOILED CABBAGE!" All of a sudden sparks shot out of its beak, and the bird's giant robotic tongue burst into flames.

What was happening?

Was it Tito's bocadillo?

Was it too hot?

Was it too spicy?

NO, not even close.

"IT'S THE FOIL!" yelled Tim, suddenly understanding. "It must be causing a short circuit."

And then, faster than you could say "boiled cabbage," Tim had a brilliant idea. He wasn't strong like Tito, but he knew just the way to get rid of the monster for good. "Do you have any more foil?" he asked, turning toward Tito.

Tito reached into his pockets and took out two big handfuls of digital foil balls. "I was saving these to play fetch with Blister," he said.

Tim smiled; the balls were perfectly shaped for what he had in mind. "How about we feed these to the hungry duckie?" he said.

Tito grinned in sudden understanding. "Let's do it!"

The foil-ball missile attack surprised the giant duck with its beak still wide open. "BOILED CABBAGE!" it screamed, but it was too late. There were more sparks, dark smoke, and suddenly . . .

KABOOM!

The whole thing exploded.

"WE DID IT!" cried Tim and Tito simultaneously, hugging each other. Tim couldn't believe it. His idea had worked! And best of all, he had managed not to worry.

But Tim's happiness didn't last.

The final explosion hadn't gone unnoticed, and high above them thousands more robotic ducks zoomed toward them. The biggest of them all was a cruise-ship-sized quacking monster that dwarfed everything else around it. And guess who sat on its head, leading the incoming charge?

Of course, it was SARA!

Tim gulped. There was nothing they could do against such a large army. They could never fight all those ducks, and they couldn't run or hide, either. He tried to be strong and hold his bubbling worries, but this was way too much to handle. WHAT IF this was the EN—

But before Tim could finish worrying about their impending doom, the ground trembled. Was it an earthquake? Tim turned around and his jaw dropped. A giant figure loomed against the gray sky, casting shadows all over the valley. At its very top, a crazy dinosaur screamed at the top of his lungs: "HERE COME THE REINFORCE-MENTS!"

CHAPTER 25

KING POOP VS. DUCKZILLA

ROAR!

It was huge.

It was swirly.

It wobbled.

It was the ultimate result of combining all of Oskar's digestive offspring—the one and only . . .

KING POOP.

And sitting atop the giant poop monster was none other than Oskar!

"It's GAME OVER, SARA!" he yelled. "Surrender now or face the wrath of my Number Two."

The earth trembled as the poop giant stumbled down the mountain to meet head-on the incoming army. Under Oskar's command, it swung its wiggly arms, swatting left and right with thunderous force.

Tim observed in awe as the robotic ducks dropped like flies!

BAM! BOOM!

"Keep going! Show them who's boss!" cheered Tito.

But just when it looked as if Oskar and his poop had changed the tide of the battle, SARA, who had stayed behind, observing the scene from atop her flying Duckzilla, finally made her move. The robotic bird glided down with flashing speed and rammed its metallic head into the poop giant's belly. **PAM!** Unable to

resist the savage charge, King Poop (and Oskar with it) shot off on a collision course with the mountaintop.

"Oh no! This is terrible. Watch out, you're going to get crushed!" yelled Tim.

"No, we won't," answered Oskar, who, using his super-brain, started to turn the situation to their advantage.

Turn thirty degrees south.

Take a deep breath and hold as much air as you can.

A bit more. Perfect!

Now raise your left leg and point your big toe forward. . . .

Following Oskar's instructions, the mass of poop hit the mountain at such a precise speed and angle that its swirly body acted like a spring. It absorbed all the energy from the impact and **BOING!** hurled back toward the enemy with ten times as much force.

"YEEHAW!" cheered Oskar as King Poop whizzed down the mountain like a cannonball.

SARA gasped. "WHAT? HOW IS THAT EVEN POSSIBLE?"

Oskar had managed to take her by surprise.

"They're going to hit us! Turn to the left, you dumb piece of flying junk!" she screamed at her robotic monster.

The duck obeyed, but Oskar had anticipated that move. **ZWOOSH!** The poop missile cut through the flying monster's wing like a knife through butter, and in one swift stroke Duckzilla went down.

"That was totally awesome! You did it!" cheered Tim, as he, Tito, and Blister ran toward Oskar, who was sliding down his giant companion. Tito cheered enthusiastically, as happy as a clam.

Tim was almost in tears, overjoyed and relieved to be done. "I can't believe it's over!"

"It's NOT," corrected Oskar. "Not yet anyway. We still have to take care of her." Oskar pointed toward the smoking remains of the flying robot.

There a familiar one-eyed figure emerged from the rubble, and her evil, maniacal laughter started to echo around the mountain.

CHAPTER 26
THE SCEPTER OF COMMAND

"I guess I should have known," said SARA, dusting off her dress. "If you want something done right, do it yourself."

SARA rummaged in her pocket and revealed something that looked like a wand. She pointed it forward and grinned. "Let's wrap this up, shall we?"

"Be careful!" yelled Tim. "That must be the Scepter of Command that the cat warned us about!"

Tim was right. SARA flicked her wand, and **ZAP!** King Poop turned into a giant pile of Jell-O that collapsed to the ground with a loud SPLOSH!

"LET'S GET OUT OF HERE!" yelled Tito as globs of the gooey substance flew left and right and a tsunami of green jelly imprisoned everything in its sticky path. Tito and Oskar managed to jump out of the way just as the gelatinous wave crashed down. Tim and Blister, however, weren't that lucky and ended up . . .

SUSPENDED IN JELL-O!

Inside his gelatinous prison, Tim couldn't see, hear, or move. He couldn't even breathe, which would have been a major problem if he hadn't been a digital character. The only useful thing Tim could do was try not to freak out. *Just stay calm. Tito and Oskar will stop her. It's going to be okay!* It was actually for the best that Tim couldn't see what was happening, because out in the open, the reality was quite different.

You see, Tito and Oskar wasted no time before launching a counterattack. Oskar on the left and Tito on the right, they charged fearlessly, hoping to overpower SARA with their speed. But they didn't. SARA flicked her wrist a second time, and **ZAP!** she froze them both in midair.

Oh, poor thing, what happened? Are you feeling kind of stuck? WAHAHAHAHA!

"Okay, the party is over. Time to go," announced SARA after she ran out of ways to tease Oskar.

"This time I should get better troops, though," she reasoned aloud. "They should be smart and capable and fashionably good-looking."

And with one more flick of her wrist, **ZAP!** an army of SARA clones driving pink pickup trucks appeared out of nowhere.

"What should we do with those four, boss?" asked one of SARA's clones, referring to Tim and his friends.

"Load the dinosaur and the strong kid onto my truck," instructed SARA. "I'll find a way to make them useful. As for the two stuck in the Jell-O . . . leave them there. I bet the big rat sheds like crazy, and the spiky kid is too much of a weakling to be a threat."

And that's how Oskar, Tito, SARA, and her clones disappeared down the mountain, leaving Tim and Blister behind.

CHAPTER 27

THE STUFF HEROES ARE MADE OF

As the minutes passed, and Tim remained STUCK in a heaping mound of Jell-O, it became more and more difficult for Tim to remain hopeful. *What's going on? It's been too long. They can't still be fighting, can they?* Tim had not forgotten Oskar's warning; he was well aware that letting his worries loose within the internet could have unpredictable consequences. However, not wanting to worry, and not worrying, are two very different things, as Tim discovered when a familiar flutter crept into his stomach. *WHAT IF Tito and Oskar have lost?*

As far as Tim's worries go, this was not that big a worry. After all, Tito and Oskar had already lost, so there wasn't much for Tim's power to change.

Still, this small worry was enough. The instant Tim worried, the green Jell-O prison started to tremble, and then to shudder, and then to shake, and then to jolt, and then . . . **POP!** The Jell-O disappeared, and Tim and Blister landed, safe and free, in a pile of playful poops.

What just happened? thought Tim, puzzled. *Did my worry do this?*

That was a great question definitely worth figuring out. However, as soon as Tim looked around, his attention shifted toward a much more urgent question.

As if in response, one of the poops tugged on Tim's arm and pointed its tiny finger toward a fleet of pink pickup trucks that were rolling down the brown block road. "DADA! DADA!" the poop said.

"DADA! DADA!" repeated all the other poops with agitation.

Tim couldn't speak Poop, but it wasn't too hard to guess what the creatures were saying. Oskar was their dad, so there was a good chance that Oskar AND Tito were somewhere in one of those trucks. "Have they been captured by SARA?" asked Tim.

"DADA! DADA!" the poops repeated with urgency.

They had. And they were begging Tim to do something about it.

"What do you want me to do?" asked Tim. "I can't rescue them. They're already halfway down the mountain. And anyway, what could I do? There's no way I can defeat SARA on my own!"

GRRRR! Tim turned around, startled by the loud grunt. It was Blister. And even though Tim couldn't speak Angry Honey Badger, either, he could also guess what the digital animal was trying to say. Here's the transcript:

What are you blabbering about, you silly human? You're not alone; you're just full of excuses! Are you really going to let your fear stop you from trying to save your friends? Don't you care about what might happen to them? Well, I do care! So you can stay here whimpering as much as you want, but I, the mighty Blister, will risk everything to save them. Even if I have to do it all by myself!

And you might be wondering, Did Blister truly say all that with a single grunt?

You bet! Who knew that honey badgers could be so expressive, right?

Tim lowered his eyes, ashamed. Blister was right. Tito was Tim's best friend, and Oskar had become kind of his friend too, so no matter how low the odds of success, he had to try to rescue them. Tim stood up and patted Blister on the head. "Thank you, buddy," he said. "Wanna do this together?"

Blister grunted a "YES!" and Tim knew what he had to do. It was crazy, and dumb, and it terrified him so much that his stomach fluttered in panic, but none of that mattered. Because despite all his worries, the fire of Tim's determination was burning brighter than ever.

CHAPTER 28
SUPER TIM

Meanwhile a line of pink pickup trucks weaved its way down the brown block road. SARA, who sat in the passenger seat of the foremost truck, was trying to decide what to do with Tito and Oskar. "I think I'll use my scepter to turn the boy into a coatrack," she announced to her clone driver. "He seems plenty sturdy, don't you think?" The clone chuckled. "But wait, I have an even better idea for the dinosaur," she continued, her single eye shining with mischief. "I will turn him into a pet turtle and feed him boiled cabbage every day!"

But SARA's evil laughter was suddenly inter-rupted when the truck braked hard and **PAM!** she smashed her big head into the windshield.

"Ouch! What are you doing?" she screamed in fury. But then she saw it. There was something thundering down the mountain at tremendous speed, about to hit the road ahead of them. Was it a loose boulder? Was it a rolling wheel of cheese?

NO, it was a very angry honey badger with a screaming kid on its back.

Tim would've preferred a cooler, braver, more heroic entrance, but his situation wasn't the most appropriate for any of that. He was scared, as scared as you can be riding a manic honey badger down a steep slope, and above all, HE WAS WORRIED. Worried that they didn't have a plan to stop SARA, worried that he would fail his friends, and worried that they were approaching the cliff side way too fast, and he hadn't the foggiest idea how to make Blister stop! Tim held tight and readied himself for all his worries to come true. Instead something incredible started to happen.

First it was the sky, which went from gray to blue, to red, to green, to full-on disco light mode, blinks and flashes and all. And then . . .

BOOM! Amazingly, one of the pink pickup trucks exploded, and the clone who had been driving it became a cat dressed in a lobster costume.

BOOM! Incredibly, another one blew up, and another clone transformed into a thin-crust pizza with extra pepperoni.

BOOM! Miraculously, a third clone turned into a yellow singing shark!

The explosions continued, on and on, and by the time Blister ground to a stop on the brown block road, SARA's army was practically gone.

BOOM! The final explosion took the last pink pickup truck, and astonishingly, Tito and Oskar became unfrozen! Tim stared in open-mouthed disbelief.

"YOU? HOW?" yelled SARA, jumping out of the truck with her Scepter of Command at the ready. "You'll pay for this. I'll turn you to DUST!"

"NOOO!" yelled Tito, launching himself forward and kicking the Scepter of Command from SARA's evil hands. But he was too late!

Tim watched in horror as the weapon's deadly ray sliced through the air, straight toward him. His stomach tightened in fear, the flutter of butterflies becoming stronger and stronger, until all of a sudden . . .

The ground shook with the impossible strength of Tim's worries. They exploded, launching an energy wave so powerful that not only did it stop the deadly ray but it returned it the way it had come . . . straight toward SARA.

SARA's eye grew big like a watermelon, and before she could say a word . . .

ZAP! The evil virtual-assistant-turned-internet-virus disappeared into a pile of dust.

The battle was over.

This time for real.

CHAPTER 29

A QUICK EXPLANATION

Tito ran toward Tim. "Are you okay?" he asked.

Tim didn't know what to say. His heart was still racing, his face was covered in cold sweat, and his legs were wobblier than a jellyfish on roller skates. On top of that, he had just survived the deadliest encounter of his life and he didn't have the faintest idea as to how. But all that aside . . . "Yes, I think I'm okay," he mumbled.

Tito sighed with relief and broke into laughter. "THAT WAS FREAKING AWESOME, TIM! You were like a superhero. When did you learn to do all that?"

Tim couldn't make sense of Tito's words. Him? A superhero? No way! He had done nothing besides howling down the mountain like a crazed monkey! "I have no idea what just happened," he admitted with a shrug.

But there was someone else who did. "I think I can explain," said Oskar, joining the two friends.

"As you might remember, everything here in the internet is made of long strings of ones and zeros called code. I'm made of code, you're made of code, and yes, that silly cat dressed like a lobster is also made of code."

"But for all this to work, the internet needs something else: logic. If 1-0-0-1-0-1-0-0-0-1-1-1 were the code for the word 'BANANA,' then it would always need to be that. If the code for 'banana' suddenly turned into something different . . . well, it would be messy! And that's precisely the effect that Tim's power has on the internet. Anytime he worries, he messes things up."

"Normally, messing the internet up could have terrible consequences, which is why I warned Tim not to do it. But it looks like we caught a lucky break.

"You see, even before we got here, SARA had already been using her Scepter of Command to mess with the internet's code. So when Tim lost control of his worries, he ended up messing up something that was already messed up . . . and guess what? He actually fixed it! Pretty neat, right? Isn't it amazing how well my plan to enter the internet worked out?"

No, it didn't! It was all pure luck!

CHAPTER 30
TIDYING UP

After Oskar's explanation, there was just

one thing left to do: tidy up.

So with the help of the Scepter of Command and an endless supply of worries, Tim, Tito, and Oskar undid all the terrible things that SARA had done and restored the internet back to its former glory.

Weeks got their weekends back.

Internet communications were restored.

And all the funny, yummy, interesting, and entertaining internet content that had been removed was brought back online. Yes, even WittyMathProblems.com.

"Well, that's about it," said Oskar after getting rid of the last boiled cabbage. "I think we're done! Should we get going?"

"Aw, man, I'm going to miss my muscles," said Tito. "¡Y a ti también, Blister!"

"I'm ready," said Tim, exhausted but proud of a job well done. For once his worries had done some good. "So . . . how do we get back to the real world?" he asked.

"Easy. We just need to press that," said Oskar, pointing to the button at the bottom of this page. "It's called the home button, and it will take us back to my lair."

Really?

Yes, come on, press it!

CHAPTER 31

BACK TO NORMAL?

-- ~~SATURDAY MONDAY~~ SATURDAY! --

Home sweet home. Tim, Tito, and Oskar were back, and even though it felt as if they had spent hours within the internet, in the real world, barely a minute had gone by. Isn't that crazy?

> It's not crazy; it's science. Time is relative. I've always said that.
>
> $e = mc^2$

"Anyway, do you know what that means?" asked Oskar. "It means that we still have the entire weekend ahead of us! What should we do next?"

Tim was exhausted and had had enough adventure for the day (and the week, and the month, and probably the year, too). "Sorry, but I need a good rest!" he said.

Tito was also tired, but not as much as he was hungry. Saturday was pancake day, and he couldn't wait to get back home for breakfast. "Sorry, but I already made plans!" he said.

Oskar, however, still had plenty of energy left. "It's okay, don't worry. I should start working on a new virtual assistant anyway!"

Tim didn't relax until Oskar promised that he wouldn't build anything else that could potentially destroy the world. However, he knew that Oskar wasn't their biggest problem.

"I have to figure out a way to block my worries. FOREVER," he said. "It's the only way to handle this dangerous power!"

"Oh my! Don't do that. That's a terrible idea!" said Oskar.

"WHY? IS IT DANGEROUS?" Tim took a deep breath and tried not to panic.

"No, of course not. But it's terribly boring! We had so much fun, thanks to your worries!"

"THERE WAS NOTHING FUN ABOUT WHAT WE JUST WENT THROUGH!" yelled Tim. Although, if he were being completely honest, he'd had a bit of fun too.

"I can't believe I'm saying this," said Tito, "but Oskar has a point. Blocking your worries would be such a waste. Sure, your power made a mess, but it was also your power that cleaned the mess up!"

"But that was a fluke!" protested Tim. "In the real world, my worries will always be bad news."

"Not necessarily," said Tito. "What if you learned to control them? We could train you! Just imagine what you could do with the power to make anything happen. You could easily become the mightiest superhero ever!"

Tim thought about it in silence. *The mightiest superhero ever?* That did sound tempting. . . .

And he had seen firsthand what his power could do. Maybe Tito was onto something. "I guess we could try," he said. "But do you really think anyone can learn to control their worries?"

"Not anyone," corrected Tito. "YOU. For you, Timothy Alexander Sullivan, NOTHING is truly impossible."

ACKNOWLEDGMENTS

I cannot express enough thanks to my wife, Jacko, for her continued support and encouragement. Without her, this book wouldn't have been possible (not even with a full bottle of Impossible Juice™). Thanks to my children, whose love for wacky bedtime stories inspired me to become a writer. Thanks to my parents as well for always believing in me.

Thanks to my agent, Gemma Cooper, and the entire team at the Bent Agency. Your passion and boundless energy are infectious. You challenged me from day one to become a better writer, and I can't thank you enough for that.

Thanks to the amazing team at Aladdin/ Simon & Schuster for all your hard work, support, and dedication. Special thanks to Karen Nagel, Jessi Smith, and Karin Paprocki. You rock! We've had so much fun over Zoom, and I can confidently say that you've made this book so much better than it was the moment we started. I'm forever thankful!

Finally, thanks to you, the reader. I hope you have enjoyed reading this book as much as I enjoyed writing and illustrating it. And to those of you who took on the challenge of solving the maze that I drew: BRAVO!

ABOUT THE AUTHOR

AXEL MAISY was born and raised in Barcelona and has lived most of his adult life in Hong Kong. He currently lives in Mill Valley, California, surrounded by magnificent redwood forests with lovely hiking trails that he wishes he'd visit more often. When he is not writing or drawing big-eyed characters, Axel spends his time watching squirrels and unsuccessfully chasing raccoons away from his vegetable garden.